USBORNE HOTSHOTS

USBORNE HOTSHOTS

JOKE BOOK

Philip Hawthorn

Edited by Mandy Ross
Designed by Fiona Johnson

Illustrated by Kim Blundell

Series editor: Judy Tatchell
Series designer: Ruth Russell

What goes Moo! Baa! Oink! Woof! Quack?

A cow that speaks five languages.

What goes "Quick! Quick!"

A duck with hiccups.

CONTENTS

Million-hare

Crow-bot

How do you hire a horse?

Make it wear stilts.

Batty books

School daze

Beaky birds

What do you call a large, angry seabird?
An alba-cross.

If a swan sings a swan song, what does a cygnet sing?
A signature tune.

What should you never do with a five-ton canary?
Argue.

What lives at the South Pole and smiles?
A pen-grin.

What do you call a failed pelican?
A pelican't.

What's the definition of illegal?
A sick bird.

And now the feather forecast.

It will rain just twice this week – once for three days and once for four.

Finish this proverb: "A bird in the hand..."

"...makes it hard to blow your nose."

Why did the dinosaur cross the road?

Because chickens didn't exist then.

Raven-mad

Buzz-ard

Where do swallows go to do their shopping?

Why do humming-birds hum?

Because they can't remember the words.

To the swooper-market.

What bird flies faster than the wind?

A hurri-crane.

10

Ducktor! Ducktor!

Your bill is enormous.
So? I'm a quack doctor.

I feel like a canary.
Just perch there and I'll tweet you in a minute.

I keep thinking I'm a joke.
Don't make me laugh.

Why is the sky high?
So that birds don't bump their heads.

What goes "Hmmm-choo"?
A humming-bird with a cold.

What will the cockatoo be on her next birthday?
Cockathree.

Why do storks stand on one leg?
Because if they lifted two they'd fall over.

What did the crow say when it laid a square egg?
Ouch.

What's black, white and red all over?
An embarrassed penguin.

Why do swallows fly south for the winter?
Because it's too far to walk.

Which seabird was a famous astrologer?

Gullileo.

My tern

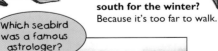

Sparrow-chute

Rook and roll

Bird of pray

Crow-cus

Turtle-dove

Coldfinch

Falcon-powder

Egg-sit

Art-gullery

King-fisher

Crow-mance

Robin-hood

Feather duster

Crane

11

Bugs galore

What do you call a spider with no legs?

A raisin.

Jitter bug

Litter bug

Buggy

Broomstick insect

Ant-artic

Eleg-ant

Scentipede

Crane fly

What's got six legs, a long tongue and makes pizzas?

A butterfly (I lied about the pizzas).

Sentry-pede

Scorpion

Scorpi-off

Why was the spider on television?

To read the webber forecast.

Mosqui-toes

BUG BOTTLE

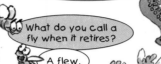

What did the caterpillar say to the butterfly?

You'll never get me up in one of those things.

What do you call a fly when it retires?

A flew.

What has antlers and bites?

A moose-quito.

What's got six legs and always does its homework?

A fly swat.

Why do bees have sticky hair?

Because they use honey combs.

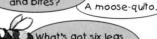

What looks like a grasshopper and wears a blue hat?

A grasshopper in a blue hat.

What do snails use to make their shells shiny?

Snail polish.

Moss-quito

12

Why was the centipede late for the soccer game?

It took her two hours to put on her boots.

What do you get if you cross...

...an elephant and a fly?
An overweight spider.

...a tennis court with a snail?
A lot older.

...a beetle and a rabbit?
Bugs bunny.

...a bee with a bun?
A hum-burger.

...a grasshopper and a hippo?
Craters in your lawn.

...a bug and a tube of glue?
A stick insect.

Waiter! Waiter!

There's no fly in my soup.

There's a beetle in my soup.
Sorry, it's the fly's day off.

My plate's wet.
That's the soup.

There's a fly in my soup.
It's OK, he wiped his feet on the bread roll.

What's this in my soup?
I don't know – all insects look the same to me.

Heard about the two tarantulas that got married?

It was a lovely webbing.

Why did the fly fly?
Because the spider spied 'er.

Which pop group do beetles like best?

The Humans.

13

16

Food frenzy

Where do bees look up facts?

In an encyclo-bee-dia.

CAKES AND BISCUITS
Evan Uther

RUNNY HONEY and other rhymes
Jean Bean and Jake Cake

POSH NOSH
Gordon Blurr

MAKING HONEY
B. Keeper

Bee-low

Bee-ware

Bee-neath

BEE KEEPING
Ivor Hive

PASTA DISHES
Ken L. Ownie and Mack O'Rownie

SUCCESS IN THE KITCHEN
Verity Licious

FISH SQUASH
Sir Dean Tyn

THINGS TO EAT WITH SOUP
Roland Butter

TOMATO SAUCE
Kate Chupp-Bottle

SALAD DRESSINGS
Vinnie Gurr and May N. Ayze

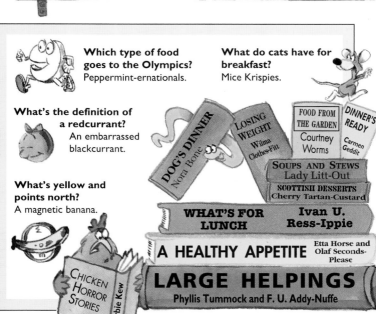

Which type of food goes to the Olympics?
Peppermint-ernationals.

What do cats have for breakfast?
Mice Krispies.

What's the definition of a redcurrant?
An embarrassed blackcurrant.

What's yellow and points north?
A magnetic banana.

DOG'S DINNER
Nora Bone

LOSING WEIGHT
Wilma Clothes-Fitt

FOOD FROM THE GARDEN
Courtney Worms

DINNER'S READY
Carmen Geddit

SOUPS AND STEWS
Lady Litt-Out

SCOTTISH DESSERTS
Cherry Tartan-Custard

WHAT'S FOR LUNCH
Ivan U. Ress-Ippie

A HEALTHY APPETITE
Etta Horse and Olaf Seconds-Please

LARGE HELPINGS
Phyllis Tummock and F. U. Addy-Nuffe

CHICKEN HORROR STORIES
Barbie Kew

17

23

25

Spaced out

Honey-moon

What do you call a space wizard?

A flying saucerer.

What sea is in space?

The galax-sea.

Why are false teeth like stars?

Because they come out at night.

How do astronauts play badminton?
With a space-shuttlecock.

Launch-box

What did the hungry astronomer say?
I'm star-ving.

What do cows say at night?

Mooooon.

When is the Moon not hungry?
When it's full.

Star-fish

Which is the most polluted planet?
Pollute-o.

What do you call a flying saucer in hot fat?
An unidentified frying object.

Egg-stra terrestrial

Austr-alien

Why is the planet Saturn like a finger?
Both have rings around them.

Ass-teroid

arking meteor

What do astronaut archers aim at?
The star-get.

How do you get a baby astronaut to sleep?

Martian-mallows

What did one shooting star say to another?
Pleased to meteor.

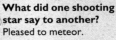

Rocket.

Why did the mouse-tronaut nibble the rocket?

Because it was in gnaw-bit.

Star-ling

27

Create your own jokes

Two meanings

You can make up lots of jokes using words that have two meanings or that sound alike. This kind of joke is called a pun.

> A pun is sometimes called a play on words.

Think of two words that sound alike: *red, read*. Then think of two things that could be described by these words (see right). Now ask why the two things are alike.

Why is a fire engine like a book?
Because they're both red (read).

A fire engine is red.

A book is read.

Here are some words with two meanings...

pen	bank	swallow
match	bill	stamp
duck	stable	nail

...and some that are spelled differently but sound the same:

right – write
weigh – way
bear – bare
hair – hare

plain – plane
tow – toe
nose – knows
tale – tail

Replacing words

Some jokes are funny because all or part of a word is replaced by another word which sounds like it. Here is how to make up this type of joke.

> What flies and stinks?

> A smelly-copter.

Think of a short word. Then think of another word that sounds similar to it:
mole, roll

Think of a phrase using the new word:
roller coaster

Swap the old word for the new word:
mole-er coaster

Think of a question that links the two ideas.

Which ride do moles like best at the fairground?
The mole-er coaster.

Here are some other ideas for puns which replace part of a word with another.

hen-chanted
Bull-garia
bee-low
hen-ergy
Fr-ants
chimp-ney

Gi-ant

Inf-ant

30

Odd combinations

Some jokes use odd combinations – objects or activities that wouldn't normally come together.

Choose an object. Think of two ways to describe it.

It flies. It has wheels.

Think of an activity it could never do.

Go on a trampoline.

Describe the activity.

Bounce up and down.

Use your three descriptions to make up the joke:

What has wheels, flies and bounces up and down?
A plane on a trampoline.

Here are more odd ideas. All you have to do is think of an odd way to describe an object and the unlikely activity it is doing.

What's (description) and goes round and round?
A (something) in a washing machine.

What's ... and laughs?
A ... reading a joke book.

What's ... and glows?
A 100 watt...

What's black and white and has eight wheels?
A penguin on roller skates.

What's the difference between...

You can make up this type of joke by finding a pair of words that make sense when you swap around their first letters.

> What's the difference between a rainstorm and a lion with toothache?

> One pours with rain and the other roars with pain.

This is called a spoonerism, after Reverend W. A. Spooner who came up with lots of them.

Obvious jokes

In these jokes, the answer is the most obvious one, which catches the other person off guard. The most famous example of this kind of joke is:

> Why did the chicken cross the road?

> To get to the other side.

Here is another example to help you start making up your own.

> What do you call a chef with a banana in each ear?

> Anything you like. He can't hear you.

What do you get if you cross...

To make this type of joke, you need to imagine a strange combination of objects and then think of a funny or clever way to describe them. Here is an example:

What do you get if you cross a joke book with a few geese?

A giggle gaggle.

You could try making a joke square. The one below has been partly filled in. Try to think of things for each blank square.

	Leopard	Hippo	Bee
Pot of glue		Stick in the mud	
Jellyfish	Spot the jellyfish		
A rose			A bee-auty

Knock! Knock! Doctor! Doctor! Waiter! Waiter!

These three kinds of jokes are easy to make up. Here are a few ideas to get you started.

Knock! Knock!
Here are some Knock! Knock! names.

Noah (Know a...)
Wilma (Will my...)
Howard (How would...)
Alison (I listen...)

Waiter! Waiter!
Try making up the waiter's reply for each of these jokes.

What's this fly doing in my soup?
Your sleeve's in my soup.
There's a dead fly in my soup.
Do you have frog's legs?

Doctor! Doctor!
What might a doctor advise?

I feel run down.
People keep disagreeing with me.
I'm afraid of the dark.
No one believes what I say any more.

Doctor, Doctor, I've a problem. Can you help me out?

OK, where did you come in?

This book uses material previously published in the *Usborne Book of Animal Jokes* and *Book of Silly Jokes*.

First published in 1996 by Usborne Publishing Ltd, Usborne House, 83-85 Saffron Hill, London EC1N 8RT, England.

First published in America March 1997. UE

Printed in Italy.